P9-CSU-768

MONSTER POEMS

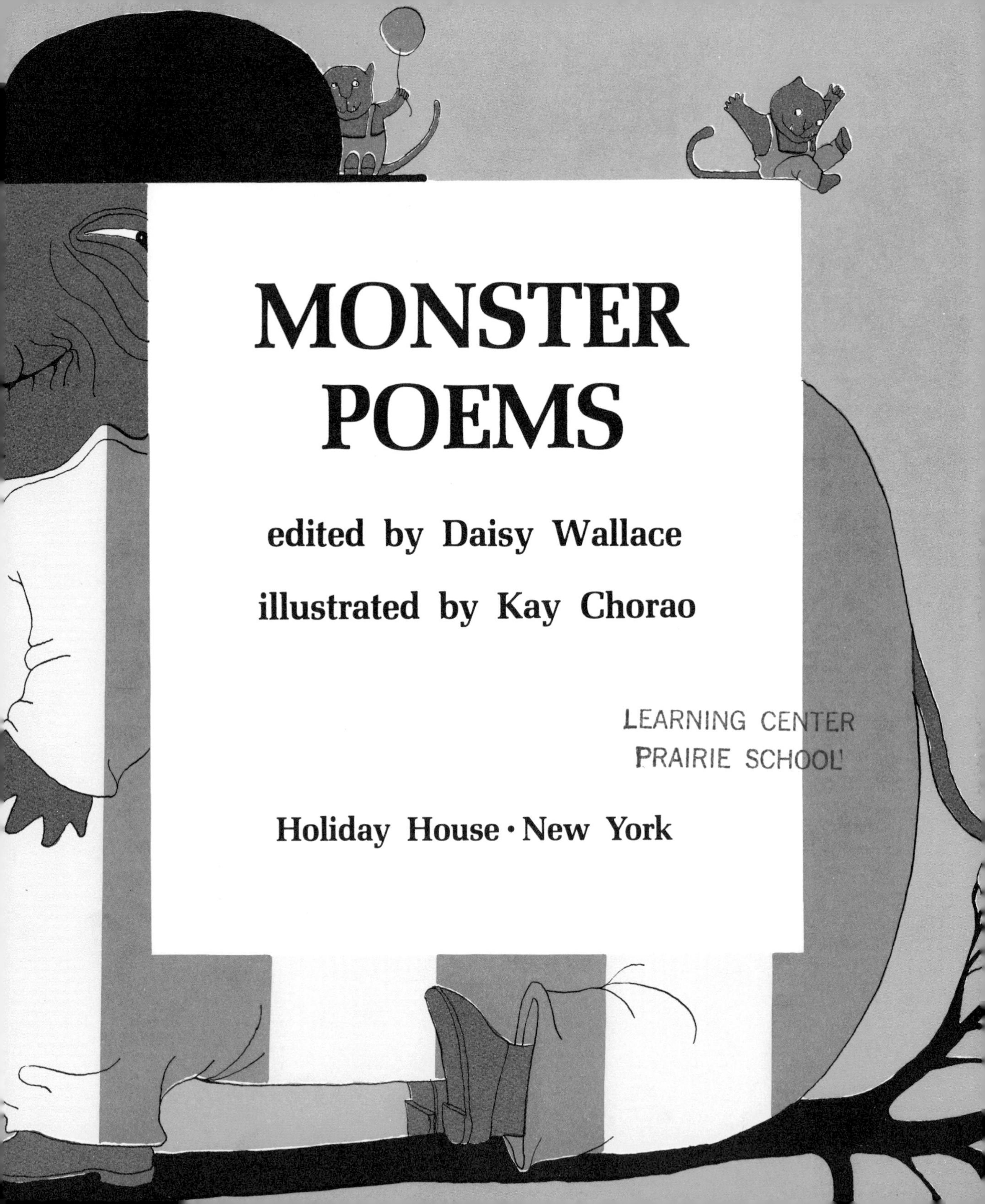

MONSTER POEMS

edited by Daisy Wallace

illustrated by Kay Chorao

Holiday House · New York

For Ashley

GRATEFUL ACKNOWLEDGMENT IS MADE TO THE FOLLOWING:

Atheneum Publishers for "The Ugstabuggle" and "The Ombley-Gombley" from *The Ombley-Gombley* by Peter Wesley-Smith. Copyright © 1969 by Peter Wesley-Smith and David Fielding.

Delacorte Press for "A Long-haired Griggle" from *Poems for Sharon's Lunch Box* by Alice Gilbert. Copyright © 1972 by Alice Gilbert.

Harper & Row, Publishers, Inc. for "The Spangled Pandemonium" from *Beyond the Pawpaw Trees* by Palmer Brown. Copyright, 1954, by Palmer Brown.

Michael Patrick Hearn for "This Thing." Copyright © 1976 by Michael Patrick Hearn.

Florence Parry Heide for "What's That?" and "Monster Menu." Copyright © 1976 by Florence Parry Heide.

Steven Kroll for "Monsters Everywhere." Copyright © 1976 by Steven Kroll.

J.B. Lippincott Company for "Please, Johnny!" from *The Man Who Sang Sillies* by John Ciardi. Copyright © 1961 by John Ciardi.

Jack Prelutsky for "Flonster Poem." Copyright © 1976 by Jack Prelutsky.

Joan Resnikoff for "The Munster Cheese Monster" by Alexander Resnikoff. Copyright © 1976 by Joan Resnikoff.

Scholastic Magazines, Inc. for "The Monster's Birthday" and "The Monster's Pet" from *Spooky Rhymes and Riddles*, text © 1972 by Lilian Moore.

Shel Silverstein for "Not Me." Copyright © 1976 by Shel Silverstein.

Elizabeth Wintrop for "The Monster in My Closet." Copyright © 1976 by Holiday House, Inc.

Library of Congress Cataloging in Publication Data

Main entry under title:

Monster poems.

SUMMARY: Seventeen poems by various authors describe different kinds of monsters.

1. Monsters—Juvenile poetry. [1. Monsters—Poetry] I. Wallace, Daisy. II. Chorao, Kay.
III. Title.
PZ8.3.M76 811'.5'4080375 75-17680
ISBN 0-8234-0268-1

CONTENTS

Ghoulies and Ghosties *Old Cornish Litany* 7

Flonster Poem *by Jack Prelutsky* 8

The Monster's Birthday *by Lilian Moore* 10

The Monster in My Closet *by Elizabeth Winthrop* 12

Please, Johnny! *by John Ciardi* 13

A Long-haired Griggle *by Alice Gilbert* 15

What's That? *by Florence Parry Heide* 16

The Ugstabuggle *by Peter Wesley-Smith* 17

The Spangled Pandemonium *by Palmer Brown* 18

The Ombley-Gombley *by Peter Wesley-Smith* 20

Not Me *by Shel Silverstein* 21

The Monster's Pet *by Lilian Moore* 23

Monster Menu *by Florence Parry Heide* 24

Monsters Everywhere *by Steven Kroll* 25

This Thing *by Michael Patrick Hearn* 27

The Munster Cheese Monster *by Alexander Resnikoff* 28

In a Dark Wood *Anonymous* 29

GHOULIES AND GHOSTIES

From ghoulies and ghosties,
Long-leggity beasties,
And things that go BUMP in the night,
Good Lord deliver us.

OLD CORNISH LITANY

FLONSTER POEM

the flime devoured the floober
and the flummie dined on flime,
the fleemie gulped the flummie down
in scarcely any time

the fleener chewed the fleemie
but in hardly half a wink,
he was swallowed by the floodoo,
who was eaten by the flink

the flink was rather careless
and was gobbled to the bone
by an enterprising flibble,
who fell victim to the flone

the floath who fed upon the flone,
soon met another floath
and while they wondered what to do

the flakker ate them both
JACK PRELUTSKY

THE MONSTER'S BIRTHDAY

Oh, what a party!
They all ate hearty
    of elegant bellyache stew.

Then came the cake
In the shape of a snake
    and trimmed with octopus goo.

The balloons all went BANG!
And everyone sang,
    "Happy birthday, dear Monster,
    to you."

LILIAN MOORE

THE MONSTER IN MY CLOSET

A monster moved into my closet
Just the other day.
He was sniffing a boot when I opened the door,
I told him to go away.
"I came for a visit," he said with a smile.
"My sister sleeps up on the shelf.
(I hope you don't mind if I chew on your shoe?)
She isn't in very good health.
She won't stay away from those ice skates,
I told her they're hard to digest.
She insisted on eating them, laces and all,
And now she needs a long rest."
The monster was gone in the morning.
His sister I never did see.
The floor of the closet was clean and bare,
Not a shoe did they leave for me.

ELIZABETH WINTHROP

PLEASE, JOHNNY!

The SHREEK is a shiverous beast.
He's as loud as a boy-and-a-half.
All other beasts shun him—at least
When he lets out that boomerous laugh.

When he whispers, it sounds like the roar
Of a train on a bridge you are under.
When he talks, it sounds very much more
Like a cave full of cannons a-thunder.

But not even the last clap of doom
Could be heard through his blabberous laugh.
Nothing human could live through its boom.
It's as loud as a boy-and-a-half.

JOHN CIARDI

A LONG-HAIRED GRIGGLE

A long-haired Griggle from the land of Grunch
Always giggled when he ate his lunch.
He'd wiggle and giggle, and munch and crunch
While nibbling the pebbles that he liked for lunch.

ALICE GILBERT

WHAT'S THAT?

What's that?
Who's there?
There's a great huge horrible *horrible*
creeping up the stair!
A huge big terrible *terrible*
with creepy crawly hair!
There's a ghastly grisly *ghastly*
with seven slimy eyes!
And flabby grabby tentacles
of a gigantic size!
He's crept into my room now,
he's leaning over me.
I wonder if he's thinking
how delicious I will be.

FLORENCE PARRY HEIDE

THE UGSTABUGGLE

Over by my bedroom wall
The Ugstabuggle stands,
A monster nearly nine feet tall
With hairy, grasping hands.
In afternoons and mornings
He's always out of sight,
But often I can see him
In the darkness late at night.
Yet when I do not think of him
He disappears again,
And when I sleep he goes, because
I cannot see him then!

PETER WESLEY-SMITH

THE SPANGLED PANDEMONIUM

The spangled pandemonium
Is missing from the zoo.
He bent the bars the barest bit,
And slithered glibly through.

He crawled across the moated wall,
He climbed the mango tree,
And when the keeper scrambled up,
He nipped him in the knee.

To all of you, a warning
Not to wander after dark,
Or if you must, make very sure
You stay out of the park.

For the spangled pandemonium
Is missing from the zoo,
And since he nipped his keeper,
He would just as soon nip you!

PALMER BROWN

THE OMBLEY-GOMBLEY

Once upon a train track
The Ombley-Gombley sat.
Rumble clang,
Jumble jang,
Crumble bang–
And that's the end of that.

PETER WESLEY-SMITH

NOT ME

The Slithergadee has crawled out of the sea.
He may catch all the others, but he
won't catch me.
No you won't catch me, old Slithergadee,
You may catch all the others, but you wo––

SHEL SILVERSTEIN

THE MONSTER'S PET

What kind of pet
Would a monster get
If a monster set
His mind on a pet?

Would it snuffle and wuffle
Or snackle and snore?
Would it slither and dither
Or rattle and roar?

Would it dribble and bribble
In manner horr-rible
Or squibble and squirm
Like a worm?

And every day
In pleasant weather,
Would they go out
For a walk together?

LILIAN MOORE

MONSTER MENU
(for when you invite a monster for lunch)

cold soup (of raw eggs)
with dumplings of mud
a beaker or two
of rancid old blood

the brains of one worm
cut in very small pieces
and fried for an hour
in three different greases

stewed gizzards of lizards
with crocodile eyes
poached pickles on toast
and buckets of flies

a steaming tureen
of octopus stew
baked bunions of witches
in bugaboo goo

FLORENCE PARRY HEIDE

MONSTERS EVERYWHERE

There are monsters everywhere,
monsters wandering in my hair,
monsters on the corner stair,
monsters in my rocking chair,
monsters going up the wall,
monsters that are very tall.
If I caught them in a bunch,
I'd have monster stew for lunch.

STEVEN KROLL

THIS THING

I found this thing the other day,
At first it didn't matter
That in delight
With ev'ry bite,
It grew a little fatter.
WELL . . .
    It swallowed my hat.
    It ate up the cat.
    It gobbled up cumquats and pears.
    It chewed on my train,
    And best model plane,
    And nibbled on tables and chairs.
    It gulped my mother,
    Sister, and brother;
    It ate them with hardly a smirk.
    And when it was through,
    It wanted me too,
    As it opened its jaws with a jerk!
BUT . . .
If its sides had been stronger,
I would be here no longer.

MICHAEL PATRICK HEARN

THE MUNSTER CHEESE MONSTER

Poor Munster Cheese Monster
He's not very frightening
But he sure does get frightened
By thunder and lightning
By wind at the window
By witches and wizards
By tigers and turtles
And spiders and lizards
By chickens and kittens
And butterflies too,
And he'd probably faint
If you mustered a "Boo!"

ALEXANDER RESNIKOFF

IN A DARK WOOD

In a dark, dark wood there was
a dark, dark house,
And in that dark, dark house there was
a dark, dark room,
And in that dark, dark room there was
a dark, dark cupboard,
And in that dark, dark cupboard there was
a dark, dark shelf,
And on that dark, dark shelf there was
a dark, dark box,
And in that dark, dark box there was . . .

A MONSTER